THAT'S GOOD! THAT'S BAD!

Margery Cuyler

pictures by David Catrow

SCHOLASTIC INC.
New York Toronto London Auckland Sydney

For Brother Gren—
that's good!   M.C.

To Hillary and D.J.—
I love you dearly.   D.C.

ISBN 0-590-45894-9

Text copyright © 1991 by Margery Cuyler.
Illustrations copyright © 1991 by David Catrow.
All rights reserved. Published by Scholastic Inc.,
730 Broadway, New York, NY 10003, by arrangement with
Henry Holt and Company, Inc.

12 11   9/9 0 1 2/0

Printed in the U.S.A.   08

First Scholastic printing, November 1992

One day a little boy went to the zoo with his mother and father. They bought him a shiny red balloon.

It lifted him high up into the sky, WOW!

The balloon drifted for miles and miles until it came to a hot, steamy jungle. It broke on the branch of a tall, prickly tree, POP!

Oh, that's bad.
No, that's good!

The little boy fell into a muddy river, SPLAT!

He climbed up onto a roly-poly hippopotamus and rode to shore, GIDDYAP!

Oh, that's good.
No, that's bad!

Ten noisy baboons were squabbling in the grass by the river. They chased the little boy up a tree until he was out of breath, PANT, PANT!

Oh, that's bad.
No, that's good!

The baboons wanted to play
vine-swing with the little boy,
WHAT FUN! The little boy
grabbed a vine and swung out
of their reach, WHEEEE!

Oh, that's good.
No, that's bad!

The vine was a big, scary snake that wiggled and jiggled and hissed, SSSSS!

Oh, that's bad.
No, that's good!

The little boy lost his grip, WHOOPS! and landed on the back of a giraffe, HOORAY!

Oh, that's good.
No, that's bad!

The giraffe leaned over to drink
some swampy water, GLUG! GLUG!
The little boy slid down its neck and fell
into some quicksand next to an elephant, SLOP!

Oh, that's bad.
No, that's good!

The elephant grabbed the little boy with its trunk
and lifted him up, up, up onto its shoulders, WHOOSH!

The elephant thumped bumpily along
to a grassy plain where it stopped
to feed. The little boy climbed down
its trunk and woke up a daddy lion
snoring in the grass, ZZZZZ!

Oh, that's bad.
No, that's good!

When the lion saw the little boy, it purred, RRRRR!
and licked the little boy's face, SLURP!

Oh, that's good.
No, that's bad!

The little boy got all wet and sticky, YUCK! and ran deeper into the jungle. It was as dark as night, OOOO! and the little boy was afraid. He sat down and started to cry, BOO-HOO!

Oh, that's bad.
No, that's good!

His tears made such a big puddle that a stork came along to have a drink, SSSSIP! It picked up the little boy with its beak, WHISH!

Oh, that's good.
No, that's bad!

The stork flew the little boy across the dark, windy sky, FLAP, FLAP! The little boy thought he would never see his parents again, SOB!

Oh, that's bad.
No, that's good!

The stork knew where it was going. It took the little
boy back to the zoo and dropped him into his parents' arms,
PLOP! His mother and father were so happy to see him,
they gave him a big hug and a big kiss, SMACK!

Oh, that's good.
No, that's GREAT!